TWO TREES

TWO TREES

**JACQUELYN HESTER COLLETON-AKINS
& ELBERT AKINS JR.**

ReadersMagnet, LLC

Two Trees
Copyright © 2021 by Jacquelyn Hester Colleton-Akins & Elbert Akins Jr.

Published in the United States of America
ISBN Paperback: 978-1-953616-48-7
ISBN eBook: 978-1-953616-49-4

This book is written to provide information and motivation to readers. Its purpose is not to render any type of psychological, legal, or professional advice of any kind. The content is the sole opinion and expression of the author, and not necessarily that of the publisher.

All rights reserved. No part of this publication may be reproduced, stored in a retrieval system or transmitted in any way by any means, electronic, mechanical, photocopy, recording or otherwise without the prior permission of the author except as provided by USA copyright law.

ReadersMagnet, LLC
10620 Treena Street, Suite 230 | San Diego, California, 92131 USA
1.619. 354. 2643 | www.readersmagnet.com

Book design copyright © 2021 by ReadersMagnet, LLC. All rights reserved.
Cover design by Ericka Obando
Interior design by Shemaryl Tampus

I dedicate this book to my children and grandchildren.

Peter Hester, and his beautiful wife Ruby Hester was blessed with nine healthy children. In this life the Heavenly Father is always seeking us as individuals who need to be saved, but the African American experience is that we are found, not in our solitariness, but in our own solidarity with those with whom we share the story and the chastening rod. Those who traveled this road together and felt that rod on their backs find in the Bible sufficient evidence the Heavenly Father elects and commissions some people to a mission only they can perform and entrusts them with his purposes for others.

TABLE OF CONTENTS

PREFACE 1

CHAPTER 1 | HUMAN RACE 3

CHAPTER 2 | YAHUWAH IS AN ISRAELITE 5

CHAPTER 3 | ST. JOHN'S RIVER. 7

CHAPTER 4 | MY DADDY'S PRAYER 8

CHAPTER 5 | DO YOU KNOW WHY?. 10

        DADDY STARTED WITH THE BEGINNING. THE CREATIONS OF HEAVEN AND EARTH 10

CHAPTER 6 | IMAGE OF YAHUWAH. 13

CHAPTER 7 | THE MARRIAGE OF ADAM AND EVE 16

        CONSUMMATE THEIR MARRIAGE 17

YAHAWAH BLESSED THE NEW COUPLE..................18

STROLLING IN THE MIDST 18

CHAPTER 8 | BEING IMPATIENT 23

CHAPTER 9 | YAHUWAH REFLECTED 25

ONE OF US.....................25

LUCIFER DECEIVES 26

THE MOTHER OF EARTH 28

THE FIRST TWINS 28

THE SEED OF SETH..............29

CHAPTER 10 | THE FALL OF MANKIND 30

PUNISHMENT AND CURSES 31

THE FLAMING SWORD 32

CHAPTER 11 | THE CURSE OF MANKIND 35

CHAPTER 12 | WHEN THE HEBREWS PROSPERED 37

CHAPTER 13 | SONS OF GOD...................39

CHAPTER 14 | DESTROYING MANKIND........41

CHAPTER 15 | NOAH COMES ON THE SCENE .. 42

	NOAH BUILDS AN ARK	42
	THE RAIN	44
CHAPTER 16 |	BABYLONIAN EXILE	46
CHAPTER 17 |	MOSES COMES ON THE SCENE	51
	THE TEN PLAGUES	52
CHAPTER 18 |	KING SOLOMON COMES ON THE SCENE	56
CHAPTER 19 |	PERSONAL STORIES	58
CHAPTER 20 |	DOCUMENTED MATERIALS	65
CHAPTER 21 |	HARRIET TUBMAN	68
	SLAVERY IN THE MILITARY	71
CHAPTER 22 |	NEW NAME	73
	LIFE OF SLAVERY	74
CHAPTER 23 |	MOVING UP IN MODERN DAY	75
CHAPTER 24 |	MY FATHER'S LAST PREDICTIONS	79
	WHAT YAHAWAH REVEALED TO ME	81
CHAPTER 25 |	THE TEN COMMANDMENTS	84

CHAPTER 26 | THE ANCIENT HISTORY OF ETHIOPIANS.................... 86

THE TWELVE TRIBES OF ISRAEL (IN ALPHABETICAL ORDER): 87

CHAPTER 27 | INSTRUCTIONS ON HOW TO BE SUCCESSFUL 89

CHAPTER 28 | CONCLUSION.....................92

HEALING FROM ABOVE 94

HEBREW CALENDAR..........................99

VOCABULARY TERMS........................ 103

DADDY'S FAVORITE SONG.................... 109

PREFACE

On December 12, 1978, my dad called me to pick him up from his rooming house on Davis Street in Jacksonville, Florida. My daddy requested to be picked up at 10:00 am and said, "Jacquelyn, bring your recorder and batteries." I informed my daddy to keep in mind that firstly, I am attending Florida Agricultural Mechanical University in Tallahassee, Florida. Secondly, I need to inform my professors of my absence on December 13th through December 15th of 1978.

Because I love my children so much, I wanted to inform my husband, Elbert. Although my children, Shelia, Shannon, and Abraham, are from my previous marriage, their wellbeing and safety was very important to Elbert and I. As a result of my daddy being sick, I took a trip to Jacksonville to take care of him. During this time, I was enrolled in my internship classes. I was also traveling to the hospital for nursing, physical education, and physical therapy so that I could teach.

CHAPTER 1

HUMAN RACE

Jacquelyn, let me explain a few things to you about planet earth and mankind. The white race made one of the biggest mistakes in history. They deceived the world to believe that Yahawah created the white humans first. Not only did the white race led the world to believe that they created the pyramids, the education system, and that they were the chosen people. They also wanted the world to believe Adam and Eve were white. The caucasians used this to make the Israelites to serve the white human race. Caucasians were the masters over the Israelites which were called Gentiles. Slavery started in early 1200 and is still going on in 2021. Because of their misleading. The white race used this to make the Israelites serve the white human race. They also made it seem logical that the Israelites came from Africa, and that we had no part in the history. Other than being a servant to the white race. One statement that would often come out of the mouth of the Edomites. Would be we will send you back to Africa, or go back to Africa where you belong.

Remember Jacquelyn. The Israelites were there from the beginning. In Genesis 1:21 we are reminded that Yahawah created man in his own image. Adam and Eve were the first Israelites the heavenly father Yahawah created; male and female. created he them. Then daddy begin to prophesize. By saying that Adam and Eve had two sons, and they were Israelites as well. Jacquelyn, keep in mind Cain killed his brother Abel. But Yahawah blessed Adam, and Eve to have another baby. And they named him Seth. Cain knew his wife, and they had a baby and named him Enoch. Enoch being a Israelite walked with Yahawah. In Genesis 6:9-10 an Israelites named Noah. Had three sons. Shem, Ham, and Japheth. From Noah, there came the human race.

Jacquelyn. Later the Israelite population changed because one of Noah's son's wife gave birth to an albino. A person with pale skin, light hair, pinkish eyes, and visual abnormalities, resulting from a hereditary inability to produce the pigment – melanin. The albinos did not like the way they looked. So the angels gave them information on how to change the appearance of their looks, forming the white race. Later, the white race changed their looks by altering their DNA to create their own image.

CHAPTER 2

YAHUWAH IS AN ISRAELITE

The Gentiles removed seventy books from the King James Version of the Bible. To name a few. Enoch, Tobit, 1 and 2 Maccabees, Song of Songs, Wisdom, Sirach, Baruch, and Books of Yahawah andYahawashi.

The Gentiles changed the Bible to keep the Israelites from learning the truth about the Jews being the "chosen" people. The twelve tribes of Israel are vital to our blood line to the Heavenly Father Yahawah, and his son Yahawashi.

The Gentiles kept us from learning, about our Heavenly Father Yahawah. Not only did they keep us from learning the truth. They made Yahawah in the image of a white man.With straight long blonde hair, blue eyes and being an edomite. Our heavenly father is not white.

In addition the Gentiles denounce our Hebrew language. They forced us to call on the name of Jesus Christ in which was their preception. They used this name instead of Yahawah the Heavenly Father and Yahawashi the Son. Who is our true Savior and deliverer of the Israelite, and for mankind.

CHAPTER 3

ST. JOHN'S RIVER

My daddy and I drove to the St. John's River, where we picked out a beautiful location to enjoy the view.

Daddy instructed me, "Let's go sit down by the river." "Would you like to go and get some breakfast first?" I asked him. He declined my offer. Instead, he informed me that Yahawah is our Father, mighty in all his ways. And that he sent his son, Yahawashi to be the living water, and food for our souls.

Therefore, Jacquelyn he said. We will not be eating or drinking earthly suppliments today. If we want power from our heavenly father Yahawah in heaven. We must fast and pray.

As we sat on the bench facing the water. With a big smile on his face. Daddy looked out into the water. He observed that the water was very blue, with whitening fish jumping in, and out of the water in harmony.

CHAPTER 4

MY DADDY'S PRAYER

Daddy hugged me and said, "Happy Birthday, daughter!" Then daddy said, "Although I do not have a birthday present for you, and I will not be giving you money. I have something for you. That is better than silver and gold."

Daddy proceeded to pray

To the heavenly Father Yahawah. I come to you in the name of our Savior your son, Yahawashi. Asking you to guide my daughter, Jacquelyn. Lead my daughter and anoint my daughter with your power from Heaven. Thank you for keeping me this long and now you are getting ready to call me home. Bless my daughter and all my children as they walk this life's journey. Help them to receive a higher education. Yahawah, in the name of Yahawashi, teach them to be obedient to the Sabbath day and humble them in all their doings. Bless all my children. Bless Jacquelyn on her birthday, because this birthday will be her last time she will see me alive. Shalom.

YAHUWAH'S PRAYER

Daddy followed his prayer with "Yahawah's Prayer":

Our Heavenly Father Yahawah, which art in heaven, hallowed be thy name. Thy kingdom come, thy will be done on Earth, as it is in heaven. Give us this day, our daily bread, and forgive us our debts, as we forgive our debtors. And lead us not into temptation, but deliver us from evil. For thine is the kingdom, the power, and the glory, forever. Shalom.

CHAPTER 5

DO YOU KNOW WHY?

Jacquelyn, daddy asked. Do you know why Israelite people went into slavery, and was cursed for four hundred years? I replied, "No, I do not."

DADDY STARTED WITH THE BEGINNING. THE CREATIONS OF HEAVEN AND EARTH

My daddy encouraged me to go back to the beginning of time. To the place where the Heavenly father Yahawah, created the heavens and the earth.

This is when my father instructed me to get his Bible and open it up to the Book of Genesis.

You need to understand the whole truth of Yahawah, Jacquelyn. All of this is true, but I want us to read it together. (Genesis 1:1-31; Genesis 2:1-25; Genesis 3:1-24) Yahawah created the heavenly space by speaking the word.

Immediately, the sun, moon, and stars appeared in space. Yahawah created the sun for our light for the day. Yahawah created the moon for our night light. Yahawah created many different kinds of beautiful stars, and one particular star is called the "Northern Star". Yahawah created the earth, and the spirit of Yahawah moved upon the face of the waters. Yahawah divided the waters which were under the firmament from the waters which were above the firmaments: and it was so.

Yahawah separated the dry land and called it earth. And in this earth Yahawah blessed the human race to have four seasons. Yahawah called the four seasons. Fall, Winter, Spring, and Summer. Yahawah then blessed the human race to use different kinds of herbs, a variety of seeds, and many different kinds of fruit trees. Yahawah saw it was good. Yahawah created water animals. The great whales, dolphins, penguins, octopus, sharks, jellyfish, shrimps, lobsters, crabs, oysters, planktons, and many different kinds of fish to eat. The animals Yahawah created include lambs, lions, giraffes, goats, bears, tigers, horses, monkeys, cheetahs, kangaroos, turtles, foxes, deers, wolves, and many more other animals that lived on the dry land. Yahawah created animals to fly in the air; eagles, falcons, ravens, bats, doves, vultures, and other animals that would fly.

Yahawah set the days in which the human race were to work, and Yahawah set one day in which the humans were to rest. Yahawah worked for five days and rested on the sixth day, and this is called the First Sabbath Day. When Yahawah planted the Garden of Eden, he placed two trees in the midst of the garden. One tree is called The Tree of

Life and the second tree is called the Tree of Knowledge of Good and Evil. Yahawah commanded Adam and Eve not to eat or touch of the Tree of Knowledge of Good and Evil. "If you eat or touch from this tree, you will surely die," Yahawah told Adam. Eve also knew not to eat from this tree.

CHAPTER 6

IMAGE OF YAHUWAH

Genesis 1:27 says, *Yahawah created man in his own image; in the image of Yahawah created he him; male and female created he them.* There went up a mist from the Earth and watered the whole face of the ground. Jacquelyn, back in those days, Yahawah had not caused it to rain upon the earth. Yahawah said that there was no man to be the keeper or name all the animals in the Garden of Eden.

In this process, Yahawah performed the first transplant surgery, creating a woman.

Yahawah formed man in his image from the dust of the ground. Yahawah squeezed the man together and breathed into his nostrils. The breath of life went into the man first and he became a living soul. The man has two chromosomes, x and y; this is called DNA (deoxyribonucleic acid), a nucleic acid that contains the genetic code. Yahawah caused a deep sleep to fall upon the man. While he slept, Yahawah took one of man's ribs and the y chromosome and made the womb-man, side by side, by using the bone marrow from the inside of one rib. Yahawah put the rib back into man and called the man Adam and breathed into the woman's nostrils, calling this living soul Eve. Now the woman has xx chromosomes and the man with xy chromosomes. The woman produces estrogen for female traits and the primary female sex hormone is to produce a healthy baby. The male, testosterone hormones is for the male trait to produce healthy sperm and to have an erection for pleasure. When a married couple has sexual intercourse, the male's penis enters in the female's vagina and loving process begins. Suddenly, the male ejaculates inside the female. The male sperm will connect to one or more of the female eggs to conceive a child.

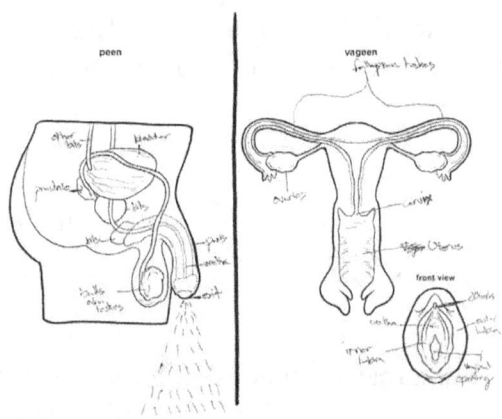

Genesis Chapter 1 verse 26, God said, Let us make man in our own image after our likeness; and let them have dominion over the air and all the things in the air. 27.God blessed Adam and Eve to be fruitful and multiply. One enjoys his beautiful wife Eve by having intercourse with her and having injaculation, when this happens this brings a possibility of reaching one of Eve's eggs because his injaculation is called the sperm. Adam's job is responsible because she was Adam's helpmate to love Adam, to have his children to be obedient to him at all times, and Adam is supposed to be obedient to Eve at all times because they are bones of my bones, flesh of my flesh. Adam 's job was to name all the animals and plants. Eve is tasked to keep the garden beautiful. She is Adam's helpmate because she is the mother of the Earth.

CHAPTER 7

THE MARRIAGE OF ADAM AND EVE

This first couple is no longer single; Adam and Eve is now married. Genesis 2:24 states, *Shall a man leave his father and his mother. The husband and wife shall cleave unto each other and they shall be one flesh.*

Adam said, "This is now bone of my bone and flesh of my flesh, because she was taken out of me."

Adam and Eve only had their Heavenly Father Yahawah, and not a mother. They were the first creation of mankind and went through a process called "The Creation". Not only did Adam and Eve evade growing nine months in a woman's womb, Cain and Abel did have to grow in Eve's womb. In today's society upon marrying, the female is given away by the father. After she conceives and carries a child for approximately nine months, she looks forward to becoming a mother.

CONSUMMATE THEIR MARRIAGE

Daddy always wanted me to know the truth about the history of Adam and Eve. That differs from what is taught in most churches, homes, and schools. So, he took time to explain all of this to me.

Jacquelyn, daddy stated. They were both naked, Adam and his wife Eve. During this time, they were not ashamed of their bodies. Once they were married, they did not consummate have sexual intercourse their union. Normally, the husband and wife consummate their marriage on their wedding night. However, Adam and Eve were satisfied and comfortable with each other. Adam felt so comfortable he did not have the instincts to have sex with Eve until he saw Lucifer had sex with his wife Eve.

Genesis Chapter 2 verse 23:
And Adam said, This is now bone of my bones, and flesh of my flesh: she shall be called Woman, because she was taken out of Man.

Genesis Chapter 3 verse 1
Now the serpent was subtil than any beast of the field which Yahawah had made.

YAHAWAH BLESSED THE NEW COUPLE

Yahawah blessed the couple and said unto them, *Be fruitful and multiply and replenish the earth and subdue it and have dominion over the fish of the sea and over the fowl of the air and over every living thing that moveth upon the earth. (Genesis 1:28)* Yahawah made it so.

STROLLING IN THE MIDST

Adam and Eve were walking together "in the midst" of the Garden of Eden on Sunday, the first day of the week. The two trees, located side by side "in the midst" of the Garden were the Tree of Life, and the Tree of knowledge (Good and Evil). In the rear of these two trees was a beautiful river. Flowing into four main rivers side by side called the Bdellium, Gihon, Hiddekel, and Euphrates. In the same area Yahawah created gold, bdellium, and onyx stone. Also, "in the midst" of the Garden of Eden was the Serpent. The Serpent was ready to use his craftiness and deception on the first man. Through deception, Lucifer told Eve that she would not die when she ate of the fruit. He also disrespected Adam by speaking to his wife without Adam's consent. This Lucifer was crafty by transforming his body to look like a man and manipulating Eve by using a cunning voice. His movement was very sly, and his two arms stretched out inviting Eve to come to him. Lucifer began putting his thoughts into words and his words into actions to deceive this couple. Just as he beguiled the first couple back then. Lucifer's mission is to deceive the whole world now. One thought that Lucifer put into action was impregnating Eve to produce his evil offspring.

When sexual intercource took place between Lucifer and Eve thorns and tussels grew all over every part of the earth.

Marriage

When a man and woman get married, the couple needs to seal their union by consummating their nuptials by having sex the day of the wedding. When a married couple has sexual intercourse, the male's penis enters the female's vagina, and a loving process begins. Suddenly the male ejaculates inside the woman. The male sperm will connect to one or more of the female eggs to conceive child.

Body Break Down

According to a national survey around the world, approximately 11,000 married men were surveyed, and 50% said they liked having sex with their partner and 50% said they did not. The problem arises when one person in the marriage does not want to have sex, and the other person wants to. 35% of men said that they would not have married their spouse if they knew their marriage would be sexless (not having sex). Only 7% of married couples have sex about 56 to 58 times in a year.

The natural decline of the reproductive hormones in women is called menopause. This stage in the female's life means that the woman's ovaries start making less estrogen and progesterone and fertility declines. Eventually, the ovaries stop producing eggs and this marks the end of the menstrual cycle or period in women. Menopause is diagnosed. This usually happens in the 40s or 50s. Symptoms leading up to menopause may include irregular periods, vaginal dryness, hot flashes, chills, night sweats, sleep problems, mood changes, weight gain, slowed metabolism, thinning hair, dry skin, psychological problems, and loss of breast fullness.

The male is responsible for the elation of PEA (Pulseless Electrical Activity). PEA is a chemical signal messenger between nerves and neuroregulator that is normally synthesized in the brain from the amino acid phenylalanine. PEA amplifies the signal strength and effectiveness of the major neurotransmitters in the human brain to improve your life. The excitement a married couple feels when they meet sexually, and the euphoria that you get when you are around the person you are sexually interested in brings PEA. PEA has invigorating, stimulating, energizing effects. PEA acts on the central nervous system to produce alertness, wakefulness, attention, energy, and endurance. This potent chemical begins to react in mind, but in three years it begins to decrease.

The hormone called testosterone begins to decline in males. This change in men occurs because of erectile dysfunction, as they get older, sexual abuse, medical conditions, generic conditions, or depression. Other cases of low testosterone are substance abuse, kidney dysfunction, blood dysfunction, smoking, alcohol, excessive coffee, not obeying the ten commandments, and observing the Sabbath Day.

In a study of men 60 to 75 years of age are going through a condition called prostate,unable to use their penis for sex and are engaging in homosexuality. These men were married and single.

Marriage Vocabulary

1. Marriage – union of two people as partners
2. Heterosexual relationship – involving sexual intercourse between individuals of opposite sex.
3. Intimacy – close familiarity
4. Important – great significance
5. Sexual desire – interest in sexual objects or activities
6. Turn off the lights – turning the lights off
7. Masturbation – stimulation of the gentles for pleasure
8. Cheating – act dishonestly
9. Shame – a painful feeling of humiliation
10. No sex tonight – no sex at all
11. Dating – two people attracted to each other
12. Loneliness – by yourself
13. Communicate – share or exchange information
14. Reality – state of things as they exist

15. Love – an intense feeling of deep affection
16. Success – accomplishment of a purpose
17. Couple – two people considered together
18. Pray together – two or more people praying to the Heavenly Father
19. Woman – adult human female
20. Man – adult human male
21. Vagina - an elastic, muscular canal with a soft, flexible lining that provides lubrication and sensation
22. Uterus - the organ in the lower body of a woman or female mammal where offspring are conceived and in which they gestate before birth; the womb
23. Penis - the male genital organ of higher vertebrates, carrying the duct for the transfer of sperm during copulation
24. Anus - the opening at the end of the alimentary canal through which solid waste matter leaves the body
25. Ovary - one of the typically paired essential female reproductive organs that produce eggs and in vertebrates female sex hormones
26. Fallopian tube - One of two long, slender tubes that connect the ovaries to the uterus.
27. Homosexual - sexually attracted to people of one's own sex
28. Lesbian – A gay woman
29. Bisexual - sexually attracted not exclusively to people of one particular gender; attracted to both men and women.

CHAPTER 8

BEING IMPATIENT

When ever daddy would tell me his long stories, and often corrected me about my impatience. Even as an adult. I had to sit still and listen quietly. Sometimes, I was not always obedient. One of those times occurred when he instructed us to go on a fast for days or even weeks at a time. This was always difficult for me, even though I tried. Daddy would also instruct us not to drink water or use the restroom while he was talking. He was preparing us to give our complete reverence to our Heavenly Father Yahawah giving him our complete mind, heart, and body. Daddy would say Jacquelyn, listen to me and stop moving around on the bench. I know you are getting exhausted but hold on, don't give up. It will get hard sometimes, and you will get distracted, but keep your mind focused.We must walk by faith and not by sight. During slavery time, these strong-minded slaves believed in Yahawah and were able to endure hardship in unsanitary conditions. They were able to survive the journey without food, water, and hygiene care.This caused the Israelites to depend upon the Heavenly Father Yahawah, with his teachings on how to fast.

I know that we arrived here at 10:00 a.m this morning, daddy said it is now 8:45 p.m in the evening. But I still have so much to tell you. I know that it is dark and hard to see some things, but we have lights to help us see.

I know your mind is thinking about something else. Keep your mind focus Jacquelyn. Stop worrying about your family! I called your husband this morning and gave him instructions. He will meet us at the Holiday Inn on Golfair Boulevard at 4:00 am on December 14, 1978. Don't worry about your stay either, I have paid the hotel bill.

I know that you did not have a chance to drink, eat or use the restroom, but I need you to continue to stay focused and listen to me. Your body needs to go through a total process of fasting and that is what you are doing. So, cheer up. You will see your children and husband very soon. Remember that this is your book. You are the author. Keep in mind your steps are ordered by our Heavenly Father Yahawah, and his son, Yahawashi.

Daddy helped me to focus by taking me for a walk beside the river. His discipline was very good for us, because I was able to bring my body under subjection to the Heavenly Father Yahawah to his will. Daddy instructed me to put another tape in the tape recorder.

CHAPTER 9

YAHUWAH REFLECTED

Jacquelyn, keep in mind that the earth was created over 7,000 times or more, and women have always made the same mistake of being deceived by the serpent.

ONE OF US

Yahawah said to the angels, "Adam and Eve is now one of us, knowing good and evil." Although he wanted Adam and Eve to eat and love each other as a couple in the garden, they did not grow in his grace and drink his everlasting water for Yahawah is the Tree of Life. Yahawah knew that if Adam and Eve ate from the Tree of Life after they had sinned, they would remain fallen forever. Hence, Yahawah drove Adam and Eve out of the Garden of Eden. Needless to say Yahawah had to punish the first humans he created. This was the result of them not obeying Yahawah's first command.

Yahawah said unto Adam, *Because you have hearkened unto the voice of Eve, your wife, and have eaten of the tree, of which I commanded you that you should not eat; cursed is the ground for your sake; in sorrow you will eat of it all the days of your life.*

As if this wasn't enough punishment for Adam, Yahawah continued, *Thorns and thistles will be with you, and you will eat the herb of the field. Sweat will run from your face. Adam and all mankind, will return back to dust.* (Genesis 3:17-18)

LUCIFER DECEIVES

Yahawah gave Adam a command that he should not eat of every tree of the garden. He commanded Adam not to eat from the Tree of the Knowledge of Good and Evil in the Garden. Yahawah said, *Of every tree of the garden you may freely eat, but of the Tree of the Knowledge of Good and Evil, you shall not eat of it; for in the day that you eat thereof you will surely die.* (Genesis 3: 2-3)

That evil and jealous (Lucifer) plotted to destroy the plan of Yahawah for mankind. Thankfully, Lucifer tried but was unsuccessful. In the end, Yahawah still won!

Eve was offered a fruit from the Tree of the Knowledge of Good and Evil by Lucifer and she responded, *'But of the fruit of the tree which is in the midst of the Garden, Yahawah hath said, Ye shall not eat of it neither shall ye touch it, lest ye die.'* (Genesis 3:3) Poor Eve did not realize that she was being manipulated. So, the Lucifer told Eve that this

Tree of Knowledge would give them as much knowledge as Yahawah. He even assured her that she would not die. Lucifer is deceptive. (Genesis 3:4)

Jacquelyn, now look at this. Lucifer planned to expose his handsome, naked body to Eve, waiting to catch her eyes. When Eve looked upon Lucifer, she found him to be pleasant to the eyes, plus he had a well-built body that was desirable. Eve was now under the influence of her flesh, and she lusted after Lucifer. She lost control and forgot about her husband. Instead of Adam rebuking Lucifer when he confronted Eve, he did not say a mumbling word. The sad thing is that Adam was beside Eve the entire time Lucifer swindled her. Adam should have quoted words from the Heavenly Father and said, "My woman and I will not eat or touch this fruit, Serpent, because we love Yahawah and will obey his voice." Instead of Adam taking a stand against Lucifer, he allowed her to be tempted by the serpent.

The serpent had no respect for Adam nor his wife. Eve had no control, because she did not discipline herself when seeing Lucifer's naked body. She even allowed him to get into her flesh.

Eve, giving into temptation, committed adultery with Lucifer. During the whole event, Adam remained silently and observed the entire act. After Eve's act of adultery with Lucifer, she made love with Adam. This is when Adam's and Eve's eyes became open to the knowledge of good and evil. They no longer felt the same because they saw themselves, the animals, and the Garden differently. The couple realized they were naked. The two of them found fig leaves and made clothing to cover up themselves and tried to hide the shamefulness of their sin.

Jacquelyn, this is what Yahawah showed me in many dreams. Adam and Eve brought the fall of mankind on our race, because they did not obey the commandments of Yahawah. He gave them his law at the beginning, but they disobeyed the Heavenly Father in the Garden of Eden by allowing the lust of her eyes to desire Lucifer.

THE MOTHER OF EARTH

Eve is the mother of all living things on Earth. In addition to naming all of the trees in the world, Eve named all the beautiful flowers as well. Eve was perhaps the most beautiful woman ever known, because Yahawah created her out of his thoughts. The Heavenly Father Yahawah is perfect. Eve was a Hebrew Israelite, even if she sinned.

THE FIRST TWINS

Jacquelyn, as a result of Adam and Eve sinning in the Garden of Eden, this shows us that the Israelites were partakers of all evil from the beginning. When Eve committed adultery with Lucifer and made love to her husband, Adam, she conceived the first twins. They named one twins, Cain and the other, Abel. Cain belonged to Lucifer and inherited his evil characteristics, while Abel belonged to Adam and inherited his good traits.

Abel offering was accepted by the Heavenly Father Yahawah. Cain offering was not accepted by the Heavenly Father Yahawah. That old Serpent child, Cain, decided to kill his brother, Abel, in the fields because he refused to offer his best to Yahawah. The first murder of man was a crime of Israelite on Israelite. As a result, Cain went out from the presence of Yahawah, and he became a fugitive and a vagabond. Cain dwelt in the Land of Nod on the east of Eden and he knew his wife and she conceived and had a son named Enoch. Sin manifested more and more.

THE SEED OF SETH

Jacquelyn, Eve felt very bad all the time because she disobeyed the Heavenly Father Yahawah. After the death of their son, Adam scolded her and she felt blamed. Eve was even ashamed to pray and talk to Yahawah. When Adam came home from working in the fields, he argued with Eve. Consequently, Eve began withdrawing from her duties as the wife. Because the devil never stopped shooting his firey dots, he laughed at Eve day and night. When the Heavenly Father Yahawah blessed Adam and Eve to come together again, Eve felt like she had purpose again. During this time, Adam and Eve conceived another child and named him Seth. Eve stated, *Yahawah appointed me another seed because Cain killed his brother Abel. (Genesis 4:25).* Eve gave birth to Seth, and thanked the Heavenly Father Yahawah for another child and another chance. The seed of Seth was the lineage that Yahawashi would be born for the salvation of mankind.

CHAPTER 10

THE FALL OF MANKIND

I was familiar with the part about Adam and Eve hearing the voice of Yahawah, while they were walking in the garden in the cool of the evening. It did seem strange when Adam and Eve hid themselves from the presence of Yahawah. Daddy decided to give me a little more wisdom and knowledge about the entire incident.

Jacquelyn, Yahawah knows everything, so why would they hide behind some bush? Here is the true story of Adam and Eve and the fall of mankind.

Yahawah created Adam and Eve in the garden and he knew exactly where they were.

Adam had the nerve to say, *"I heard your voice in the garden, and I was afraid because I was naked, so I hid." (Genesis 3:10)*

What he should have said was that he saw his wife having sex with Lucifer. Instead of stopping Eve, Adam joined in being disobedient. Adam became scared of what Yahawah would say or do.

Yahawah asked, *"Who told you that you were naked? Have you eaten of the tree that I commanded you not to eat from?" (Genesis 3:11)*

Adam responded, "The woman you gave me influenced my actions."

Jacquelyn, Adam was shifting the blame to the woman. Then, he had the nerve to tell Yahawah that it was the woman that was given to him.

Yahawah said to the woman, *"What is this that you have done, woman?"*

The woman said, *"The serpent beguiled me and I did eat."(Genesis 3:11)*

The serpent deceived Eve to eat from the tree and deceived her to have sex with him.

PUNISHMENT AND CURSES

Yahawah said unto Lucifer, "Because you have done this sinful act, you are cursed above all cattle and above every beast of the field; Lucifer you shall crawl upon your belly and you will eat dust all the days of your life. There shall be enmity between two seeds, good and evil." (Genesis 3:14-15)

The good news, Jacquelyn, is that our Savior came down through the bloodline of Adam and Eve and his name is Yahawashi and he will fight against Lucifer in Armageddon.

Yahawah said unto Eve, *"I will greatly multiply your sorrow and your conception; you will bring forth children with pain and suffering." (Genesis 3:16)*

Now, Eve and all women would desire their husbands, and he would rule over the woman in marriage.

THE FLAMING SWORD

Yahawah placed cherubims (angels), holding flaming swords (fire) which turned every way, to protect the Tree of Life. Because it was located at the east of the Garden of Eden, Yahawah knew Adam and Eve would have tried to eat from this tree. He loved them and us so much that he protected them from being in a fallen state forever.

The Critical Moments of Life

Sin had now come into the world. Here you find a list of catastrophic events that were brought forth by sin:

1. Instead of obeying the Heavenly Father's command not to touch or eat the Tree of Knowledge of Good and Evil (which meant not to make love to another human being), Adam and Eve chose not to obey Yahawah.

2. Eve and Lucifer were having sex, while Eve was a virgin and married.
3. Cain killed his brother Abel.
4. Thorns, thistles, weeds, tear, vines, and animals are no longer in harmony; and man is no longer in accord with the animals.
5. Gold, silver, diamonds, and others precious gems were no longer pure. The earth started to decay. The air and water were no longer pure, but polluted.
6. Sickness in males (PEA in the brain dysfunction) Prostate dysfunction.
7. Female Menstrual Cycle
8. Menopause dysfunction
9. Declining of bone marrow
10. Husband no longer interested in their wife
11. Women were no longer interested in their husband
12. The marriage is built on one person who believes in Yahawah and his son Yahawashi, and the other thinks in alignment with the Gentiles way.
13. A person spends his/her whole life looking to get married to the person that they are in love with only to realize that was not the one the Heavenly Father Yahawah wanted them to be with.
14. In this period couples are swapping with one another. Then returning home to their spouse thinking that the Heavenly Father is pleased.
15. Women with women and men with men.

16. Different churches are having single night gatherings fun times instead of revivals and bible studies. They have stomp down bedtime.

17. Going out to dinner with your husband and other couples, and other couples are stroking you with his feet with shoes off with toes trying to provoke you.

18. Men are into masturbation at work and home.

19. Women are into masturbation at work and home.

20. In the early A.D, B.C, and moving into this time man has progressed using a play toy for sex, animals for sex, and now they are using I-robots for sex instead of a real human being. Instead of getting married to a real human being (a man or woman), they prefer to purchase an I – robot for their pleasure. Some like to use a hologram for his or her desire. We are now in end times.

Everything is coming to an end! Our devices for pleasure are more breath – taking then ever. The human race is giving up their souls for comfort, a beautiful body or just the promise to live forever. This pleasure is called human sleeves. Sin has come a along way from the Garden of Eden. Adam never did get a chance to penetrate his virgin wife first by eating of the Tree of life because Lucifer was waiting right there to persuade the word of the Heavenly Father from the heart of Eve. This married couple was told from the beginning but failed to hold on to the words of the Heavenly Father or his words from the Holy Bible. A man should stand his ground and be a man and protect his woman no matter what.

CHAPTER 11

THE CURSE OF MANKIND

Jacquelyn, Adam and Eve were cursed for the rest of their lives and this is why the Israelites went into slavery and had to serve the Gentiles and others. As generations have progressed, they have been cursed along with the Israelites. Our Hebrew people were separated from their families. As it was, slavery separated husbands, wives, children, and relatives. As a result of sin and disobedience, the Israelites had to travel different journeys across the water and land as enslaved people. During their journey, our brothers and sisters served and were raped, sold, and degraded by our Gentiles masters. Our newborn babies, as young as one to seven months, were used for alligator bait, sold to other nations, or killed without cause. Slaves lost their inheritance, their language, and their dignity to be crossbred with other races and formed new DNA. The Israelite people had to work without any wages.

They were put in iron chains and taken to the bottom of the ship, as they carried were across the ocean. It was not a pretty or pleasant thing being piled on the ship like animals. After traveling this long voyage for months, the Gentiles fed them like livestock. When the ship stopped, the Gentiles paraded them on a platform on the top deck and held them down like beasts. They stood before other humans while they called us and treated us like property. These women became pregnant from strange men. Their daughters, as early as three years old, were raped. Even their sons were raped as young as three. Those nonconforming Israelites were beat on our backs with a whip, just like our Savior, Yahawashi. No matter the season or weather (hot, cold, snow or rain), they had to remain out in the open until they dropped or passed out. Our names were taken from us and we were given Gentile names. Our ancestors worked from sunup to sundown.

CHAPTER 12

WHEN THE HEBREWS PROSPERED

Jacquelyn, you must know that before the Hebrew people were enslaved, they were full of power and authority. Our people began as kings and queens over many lands. They lived in fine homes, had high-ranking jobs such as doctors, architects, hieroglyphic writers, mathematicians, and engineers. It was within the Israelites that we would found medical doctors and pharmacists, philosophers, authors, biologists, scientists, physicists, artists, plastic surgeons, bone specialists, athletes, potters, hair stylists, makeup stylists, musicians, actors, inventors, chefs, dentists, tax collectors, teachers of Christianity, caretakers, nurses, emperors, preachers and ministers, politicians, scholars, judges, and so many significant careers that made our land rich and prosperous. The Israelites built pyramids, large building structures and monuments, and water systems. They mummified the deceased, grew large agricultural areas, made the best wines, and invented the best medicine. The Israelites made expensive furniture like cribs, Pharaoh's special bed, fine jewelry, afro combs and designer wigs for males and females. They designed and created the educational systems, the maps of the world, expensive clothing and shoes, pottery, and many more inventions.

Jacquelyn, some of the most important traits the Israelites possessed were in mental and physical skills such as bravery, speed, and combat. These men and boys fought during the ancient time in Egypt. One of their famous victories was winning over the British army. The Shaka Zulu established themselves with power as early as 500 B.C to 1828. They persevered through it all.

CHAPTER 13

SONS OF GOD

Jacquelyn, did you know that there were and still are giants on the earth? This was a result of more sin. The sons of God were the two hundred angels who came down from Heaven. They saw the daughters of men, people on earth, that were beautiful and nicely built. These daughters forgot Yahawah sent two hundred angels down to earth to help mankind build houses and develop landscape. These angels were not supposed to be lovers but helpers. Instead, these angels began to lust after the earthly women. By their own choosing, they took them as wives, and the daughters accepted them as husbands. The angels and their new wives began having babies. As these babies grew, they became giants in the land.

Let us look at how the giants caused confusion and disharmony on earth with the animals, humans, and the sons of God. These fallen angels and their offspring possessed wisdom, knowledge, and understanding. They were highly gifted, intelligent, and had super strength.

With giants in the land now, the ecosystem was thrown off. Catastrophe took place on earth. The angels and their giant babies were eating and killing everything in sight. Their high IQ spilled over to them teaching their wives black magic, sorcery, witchcraft, the horoscope, weapons to kill, beasteality, and other sinful acts. In addition to these unholy deeds, they practiced cloning and shift changing into reptilians.

The angels also taught them to be powerful like the devil by serving him and not Yahawah. Yahawah saw every imagination of the human mind. The human heart had become evil and perverted with massive violence. It grieved Yahawah to his heart that he made man. He said that he would destroy man whom he created from the face of the earth, both man and beast and all the creepy things and the fowls of the air. And he did just that.

Yahawah said in *Genesis 6:3*, *"My spirit shall not always strive with man, for that he also is flesh."* That was when Yahawah numbered their days to a hundred and twenty years.

CHAPTER 14

DESTROYING MANKIND

Jacquelyn, during this time, the earth was corrupt before Yahawah. The earth was filled with violence, sorcery, perversion, witchcraft, and idolatry. The Israelites started serving other gods and not praising the most high-- Yahawah. Hebrews were bowing down to these gods and fornicating with the animals, changing their DNA, and building cities for the future calling it Atlantic.

Jacquelyn, count the passages in the Bible and see how many times Yahawah mentioned destroying the earth. I counted six passages. Before man became sinful, Yahawah planned for mankind to live and not die. Adam and Eve were given a choice to obey or disobey. Because they disobeyed, sin multiplied and spread rapidly throughout the land. Yahawah realized that he needed to destroy the wicked people and all the animals of the earth.

CHAPTER 15

NOAH COMES ON THE SCENE

Noah, the Hebrew Israelite, found grace in the eyes of Yahawah. He had a wife, sons, and daughters-in-law. Noah walked uprightly with Yahawah day in and day out. He was the only just man with a perfect heart living in his generation. Daddy proceeded to explain how Noah came on the scene.

NOAH BUILDS AN ARK

Jacquelyn, during this time, it never rained on earth, just a midst from the ground. Yahawah caused vapor to come upon the land for moisture. So, when Noah told the people it was going to rain, and they needed to repent, they did not believe him. In the meantime, Yahawah told Noah to build an ark with gopher wood. He instructed Noah exactly how he wanted the ark to look inside. There were rooms in the ark and they were covered with asphalt within and without. The ark was fashioned about three hundred cubits (450 feet) in length, fifty cubits (75 feet) in width, and thirty cubits (45 feet) in height. There was a window within the ark about a cubit (1.5 feet) with a door on the side. Noah built a three-story ark to include the animals of every size and shape.

Once Noah built the ark, he and his family of eight were the only people saved. Therefore there were no grandmothers, no grandfathers, no in laws, no cousins, no uncles, no aunts, no nephews, no nieces, or no other humans saved. Then, Noah brought in two of every clean animals into the ark. Along with Noah and his family, these animals were considered precious cargo.

This part is crucial, Jacquelyn, because Noah and his family had to collect everything they needed to sustain them and the animals in the ark until the water had subsided. It was important for the women to prepare nutritious meals for everyone. They needed to include different kinds of food, plants, water, milk, barley, wheat, seeds, soap to clean the body, empty buckets, plates, silverware, bowls, cups to drink, herbs and spices for medicine, olive oil, fruit trees, ripen fruit, nuts, clean clothing and things to sleep on, and many other things. The women had to remember to feed the animals because Yahawah sealed the ark door and they were not able to go to the market and shop for food.

Noah's Ark rested on the highest Mountains of Ararat in Turkey after the Great Flood. Eight members of Noah's family was saved. There were two of every animals, plants, and flowers that was saved.

THE RAIN

Noah preached the word to the Israelites and Gentiles:

It's going to rain! It's going to rain! It's going to rain! It's going to rain! It's going to rain! It's going to rain! Come on in the ark, my brothers and sisters and stop living in sin. Stop selling your soul to the devil. Stop serving those other gods.

From the beginning of building the ark until the end, Noah preached to his brothers and sisters. The Israelites and Gentiles, alike, made a mockery of Noah and his family. Yahawah began preparing the earth to be sealed to keep the water from evaporating from the earth. Then, suddenly there came a drop. Drop after drop, the gates of Heaven opened and the water came down and filled the earth for the first time. As the water rose higher and higher, you could hear the people outside screaming for help and knocking on the door of the ark. They asked Noah to save their children and mothers. They made it known that they were kings, sorcerers, and physicians. Some even told Noah to let them in, because they were rich and powerful. Screams could be heard, "Don't let us die, because you need us!"

Jacquelyn, these people belonged to our race and they were called Hebrew Israelites.

CHAPTER 16

BABYLONIAN EXILE

The Hebrew Israelites were surprised that the Gentiles in Egypt used all measures of force to take control and bring down their race. The Hebrew people were unable to prevail, because Yahawah warned them that they would become slaves to the Gentiles if they disobeyed. As a result of the Gentiles using all measures of force to destroy the Israelites, they captured emperors, kings, queens, doctors, and lawyers. The leaders in charge during this time were Alexander the Great, Pharaoh, and Rameses. All Israelites, especially the Twelve Tribes of Judah, were sold by their own race. These Twelve Tribes of Judah are Reuben, Judah, Gad, Issachar, Zebulon, Dan, Naphtali, Gad, Manasseh, Simeon, Levi, Joseph, and Benjamin. In their quest for power, some Israelites were sold into slavery. The slavers changed the Israelites' names to compound words as if they were livestock. Because of their sin, they became like livestock to all nations. Slaves had no power, no authority, and rarely none of them understood the truth behind slavery.

Then, my Daddy began to talk about when our planet earth became a horrible, painful, cruel, evil, and bitter land over seven hundred thousand years ago. The Hebrew Israelites, including the Twelve Tribes of Judah, went into exile. This was an act of cruelty like the Holocaust in Germany, which was one of the worst kinds of injustice on mankind. The Kingdom of Judah was sold into slavery from West Africa. The Levi Tribe took part in selling their own people, along with the French, Arabs, Palestinians, Portuguese, and Greeks.

Jacquelyn, your great, great grandfather began passing down family history to keep a record in the minds of our kin folks. During that time, the Hebrew Israelites were not allowed to read, write, and speak Hebrew, which was their own dialect. When your great, great grandfather was a young boy, he was taken from his home in Benny Port Island and placed on a large ship. They put him down in the bottom of this hell with his legs and neck in shackles. He was forced to lay on his back in his and in others' feces, urine, and vomit, which moved, bounced, and turned along with the ship. There were people above him and whenever they urinated or had a bowel movement, it came down on his face and all over him. Following these inhumane conditions, maggots grew over everyone's body. There were even stories that the back of these enslaved people's bodies were covered with sores and maggots, while some were barely alive. A lot of people died and there was a horrific odor lingering, because everyone was locked down at the bottom of the ship for months. When the masters over the ship came to feed the

Israelites, they would collect and empty large tubs of feces from around the Israelites and dump it into the ocean.

When feeding times occurred, they would put food in the same bucket and use the same scoop to distribute to the Israelites. When they refused to eat, they would come and loosen the shackles and force them to eat the unclean food. Later, in the evening time, the masters of the ship would release about forty to fifty Israelites and take them on deck, making them dance. Your great, great grandfather was unaware of the time, but usually, there would be light when they started and darkness when they returned.

Your great, great grandfather was a survivor and a man of Yahawah, who believed and had the faith of a mustard seed. Jacquelyn, let me pause so all this history can sink in and empower you.

He then got up and stood by the rail and looked at the water. He stood there for fifteen minutes before he told me to close my eyes for another fifteen minutes. I stayed seated with tears running down my face. After that time was over, he began by asking me if I knew why the Israelites suffered through slavery and hell. I told him that I was unsure. He then proceeded to tell me that when my brother, sister and I were small and growing up, we were not ready for this information. The pause was over and Daddy continued.

Jacquelyn, let me take you back and maybe you will get it. You may open your eyes naturally and also, hopefully to the spiritual and worldly knowledge. Keep in mind, the Bible was changed into many lies and the church was not taught to call our Heavenly Father, Yahawah. We are Israelites from the tribes of Judah. We are Hebrews and the light to this world to all mankind. Ruby, your mother, and I never used names like Jesus Christ, because I learned as a young boy from my mother and father that Yahawah and Yahawashi is our Father and Son. Black people always knew the real name of our Heavenly Father and his Son, but the Gentiles would beat or kill us if we used those names.

Jacquelyn, let me describe what was passed down through life. The world kept the Israelites from learning about our history and where we came from. The Bible provided us with a small portion of information about our past such as, the Israelites suffered because our ancestors, Adam and Eve, sinned at the beginning.

Jacquelyn, it will take millions of years to discuss all the horrible things we have been through in our history, but here is what I can talk about.

The Atlantic Slave Trade had the worst slave ships designed to capture, steal, and trick the Israelite people to be enslaved while making money off of them, dead or alive. It has been estimated that 35 to 55 million Israelites were sold after they reached American soil. Benny Port Island, West Africa became a hot spot where they captured Israelites, because the population was booming. In this area, the Tribe of Judah migrated to this area and throughout the whole process of slavery.

At the beginning in Egypt when the Israelites were going into exile, Pharaoh and Rameses did not give the Israelites any respect or have mercy on them. Their first order was to stop the multiplying of the Israelite babies. When midwives delivered the Israelite babies, she was ordered to kill the male and keep the female alive. When the midwives refused to obey Rameses but obeyed Yahawah instead, he ordered all male babies to be thrown over the mountain.

Slave ships were large cargo ships specially built or converted from the 17th to the 19th century for transporting slaves. Such ships were also known as "Guineamen" because the trade involved human trafficking to and from the Guinea coast in West Africa.

CHAPTER 17

MOSES COMES ON THE SCENE

During this time, Moses came onto the scene. Since Moses was a goodly and kind hearted, obedient, child, his mother was able to hide him so that he was not discovered by Rameses. So, Moses' mother made a basket and pushed him in the river. With Moses' sister looking on, Pharaoh's sister found him and had compassion. Although Pharaoh's sister reared him in the palace as her own, Moses was weaned by his birth mother and was taught the truth about his people. Growing up in Pharaoh's palace as a rich child gave Moses a different scene. So, it took Moses forty years to be clean from his lifestyle as an Egyptian. Yahawah could use him, because his mother planted a seed and Moses was born to be the deliverer. Keep in mind, Jacquelyn, these Israelites were a disobedient group of people, but Yahawah is faithful. He delivered them from the ten plagues of Egypt which consisted of blood, frogs, lice, flies, beasts, boils, hail, locusts, darkness, and death of the first-born child.

THE TEN PLAGUES

These ten plagues were only sent to the Egyptian people. Moses took his staff and turned all the rivers and water into **blood**. When this took place, all of the fish in the river died and gave a rotten odor. This odor represented how the Egyptians lived and treated the Israelites.

The **frogs** represented false prophets in the church. When the preachers opened their mouths, all of these spirits represented false teaching that would keep the people from learning and receiving the true message.

Lice represented lies, folly, hate, or no love toward people. Lice are in every lifestyle and all over our bodies.

Flies represented poor behavior, falling deeply in sin, folly, being confused, crying that no one loves me, marriage that doesn't work, losing a job, the church not helping, the body consisting of parasites in the head and body, not knowing who to turn to for help, and thoughts of committing suicide.

Beasts were the people that took on animal characteristics by naming themselves after animals. For example, calling themselves a fox, and denouncing their real name. They sought an escape by crying out for help and seeking how to become saved.

Boils represented moving away from old habits, old customs, old favored clothing, seeking new friends, thinking about coming out of the church, and being under rulers or a king. This person seeks a new life and he examines what he has experienced in life.

Hail represented Yahawah calling them to begin to hear his voice and they would know he is a new life. Because they called on the true Heavenly Father, they got saved, sanctified, filled with the Holy Ghost, and baptized in Yahawah's and Yahawashi's names.

Locust represented hearing the true word, living the word, speaking the word to others, and for the first time, feeling free.

Darkness represented the person being able to walk through the shadows of death, problem-solving, dealing with frustration, no longer smoking, drinking, or using drugs, committing adultery, no longer having idols, following the traditions of the world, and serving pagan gods. For example: no longer participating in New Year's Day, Valentine's Day, President's Day, Groundhog Day, Easter/Passover/Good Friday, Mother's Day, Father's Day, Independence Day, Labor Day, Halloween, Thanksgiving, Christmas. All of these are pagan holidays in which people feel free to participate in the traditions that have been passed down throughout this world.

The **death of the first-born son** represented the first sin that came into their lives because Yahawah formed man from the dust of the earth. The woman was built from the bone marrow of the man's rib. Male and female took it upon themselves to put sin in their lives at the beginning that grew into a lack of ego, telling lies, walking around miserable, murdering, using different kinds of drugs, doubting our Savior, being confused, and walking around like robots. Living with all the plagues in the body that was passed down from Egypt, caused it to be cursed.

Jacquelyn, now that I have reflected on what I have done in my life, I am no longer under the curse of the plagues. I am free. I thank my Heavenly Father for bringing me out of Egypt, spiritually, mentally, and physically.

The Ethiopian Israelites forgot where Yahawah brought them from, and they kept on mumbling and complaining. Then, they had the nerve to say that they wished they were still in Egypt, because they had food to eat and water to drink.

Now Jacquelyn, while these Israelites were in the wilderness, Yahawah guided them day and night, but they were so impatient. Everything had to come quickly for them. For their first meal in the wilderness, Yahawah fed them mammals from heaven and they still complained. These Israelites still refused to obey and stand still to see the salvation of Yahawah.

Jacquelyn, if you open your Bible to *Leviticus 23:1-14; 24:1-9; 26:1-3*, you will see the law of the Sabbath Day.

Ye shall make you no idols nor graven image, neither rear you up a standing image, neither shall ye set up any image of stone in your land, to bow down unto it; for I am Yahawah. Ye shall keep my sabbaths, and reverence my sanctuary;

I am Yahawah. If ye walk in my statutes, and keep my commandments, and do them...

The Heavenly Father, Yahawah, asked us to obey the Sabbath Day by informing us that we should work six days and rest on the seventh day.

Jacquelyn, encourage the people to read this information for themselves. Yahawah commanded his people to obey the Ten Commandments and all of his statues.

CHAPTER 18

KING SOLOMON COMES ON THE SCENE

Jacquelyn, let me talk about idolatry. This indeed is a true story. His name was Solomon and he was a wise king who Yahawah blessed abundantly. Solomon served Yahawah and called on Him for everything he needed in his early days as king. He even built temples for Yahawah's service.

Now Jacquelyn, he had everything, including a bad sin--he loved strange women. Solomon had seven hundred wives and princesses and three hundred concubines. One of those women was the daughter of Pharaoh. She was a Moabite woman. This Moabitess, along with his wives, turned Solomon's heart and mind away from Yahawah. Consequently, this led him to serve Lucifer. These women consisted of the Ammonites, Edomites, Zidionians, and Hittites. The Heavenly Father instructed and commanded the children of Israel not to marry or give away to marry to any these nationalities. Solomon clave to these sinful women anyway and did abominable things. For example, he built the idol god, Molech, to sacrifice small children and burn incense. Instead of sacrificing to Yahawah, Solomon made sacrifices to his wives gods. This is what Yahawah calls idolatry.

In the Hebrew Bible, Moloch is presented as a foreign deity who was at times illegitimately given a place in Israel's worship as a result of the syncretistic policies of certain apostate kings. The laws given to Moses by God expressly forbade the Jews to do what was done in Egypt or in Canaan.

CHAPTER 19

PERSONAL STORIES

Jacquelyn, these stories are personal and I want you to know about them. The first story involves two strangers, three of my children (you, Gloria, and Terry), and myself as the victim. Down through the years, I kept journals, articles, and birth records of my family. It started on November 18, 1954 when I took your mother, Ruby, to the midwife's house on Delwood Street in Mixon Town. It was there that she gave birth to a beautiful baby girl that weighed six pounds and four ounces at 12:07 am. While you and Ruby were resting, I kissed the two of you and started walking home on McCoy Boulevard. As I approached the underground bridge, I saw two men standing in the middle of the road. So, I decided to walk past them quickly, but they stopped me by saying, "Peter, Peter! Give us your new born baby."

I told them to go back to hell where they came from. When I arrived at my home, I got in and locked the doors. I sat down and thought about those two men and what they were asking me to do. The only thing I could do was pray the Lord's prayer, in Yahawah's name.

Jacquelyn, every night I always drank from "My Lady," the alcohol bottle. These two men had me concerned about my family and my children's future. However, on this particular night, I did not need that alcohol. After realizing that these men were really trying to destroy my family, I needed to get focused on the Heavenly Father. Instead of drinking this alcohol, I needed to stay sober to protect my family. This meant giving my life totally to Yahawah and being real about my salvation. This is when I received relief from worrying about my family. Knowing that Yahawah is in total control of my life and my family, I went on to work, trusting the Heavenly Father to protect them.

Jacquelyn, let me tell you another story. This story picks up where your mother and I broke up and were living in separate housing. At that time, I lived on the corner of State and Davis Street above the TipTop Bar upstairs. After work, I stopped by the TipTop Bar and brought "My Lady" and went outside. As I sat on a box, and enjoyed "My Lady". I looked up and saw the same two men approaching me. They pulled me off the boxes by my two legs.

They asked, "Don't you remember us?"

I told them that of course I did. Then, one of the men yelled out, "Give us your three children and we will give you lots of money for the rest of your life."

I told them to get thee hence, Satan. It is written that I shall worship Yahawah and only him shall I serve. Then Jacquelyn, I observed their faces as they turned green along with their hands and long fingernails. I told those animals that I would never give them my children, because I love them. After I yelled at them the two men disappeared. All of the money in the world would not cause me to give my children to a race like theirs or any other race.

Jacquelyn, this next story involves you. When you were just one year old, your godmother kept you one day, because Ruby and I had to take care of business in town. It was Wednesday, January 18, 1956, when your godmother, Ms. Bitty, babysat you, Sue Ann, and Boo Boo. During lunch, Ms. Bitty fed you mashed potatoes with gravy and English peas. After lunch, she mixed kerosene in your milk. When we arrived back home, Sue Ann was crying and saying that something was wrong with you. Boo Boo told us that you were choking. We rushed you to the hospital (Duval Medical Center), where your mother informed the nurse that your mouth smelled like kerosene and you were turning blue. The nurse took you to the back and began pumping your stomach, removing everything out. The doctor told us that your heart stopped, causing you to pass out, and they had to perform Cardio-Pulmonary Resuscitation (CPR). This resulted in you going in a coma. I had to control your mother because of her hysterical crying and carrying on. She was pregnant with George Ann, so I had to make sure she stayed calm. The doctor then put you in the intensive care unit (ICU). Finally, May 21, four months later, you came out of the coma. Everyone was in the room when you got up and stood on your own legs and said "Dada, Mama. Macaroni, Macaroni."

The doctor ordered the nurse to put in an order for macaroni and cheese and mashed potatoes with gravy. We observed you while you ate everything on the tray, except drink the milk. You picked it up in your right hand and threw it on the floor. You never drank milk again. Ruby and I discussed Ms. Bitty, but we never heard or saw from her again. All her personal things just vanished.

Jacquelyn, here comes another story. I know that you and Abraham got married, because you became pregnant. When the time came for you to have the baby, Abraham took you to Duval Medical Center, where you had difficulties delivering your first child. You eventually delivered a beautiful baby girl and Abraham named her Sheila. About thirty minutes later after the delivery, you went into a coma with a high fever and remained in that state for three weeks. Your husband, Abraham, had to go to work, but I stayed at the hospital the whole time you were there. When you came out of your coma, you called the name of Yahawashi.

Jacquelyn, I have another story. On May 12, 1977, I had one of my rooming buddies take me to Jack's Liquor Store on Merill Avenue to get "My Lady". I came back to my rooming house, a new house right across from the Ritz Theatre. I had been living there for two weeks. On this particular day, it was nice and sunny, and I decided to stay downstairs and enjoy "My Lady" under the sun. I saw some boxes by the tree, so I went and sat on them. I drank half of "My Lady" when I saw those two men coming yet again. One of them said, "Now all of your babies are here, and they are no longer babies. Give us consent to take them."

I got up calling on Yahawashi. I told them once again to get thee hence behind me, Satan, because it is written that I shall only worship Yahawah and only Him shall I serve. Those two men began to kick and beat me until I passed out.

When I came through, it was dark. This was the straw that broke the camel's back. I got on my knees and asked the Heavenly Father to take this taste of alcohol from me. I prayed that Yahawah would save my soul and deliver me from those demons. I began to call with all my power and might, asking Yahawah to please save my soul and deliver me from living in hell. Before I knew it, I was jumping around, up and down, feeling light as a feather and free. I took "My Lady" upstairs with me and washed it out. From that day to this, that alcohol bottle became a memorial. The only thing I drank from that bottle was apple juice.

After being saved, I told Yahawashi I needed a Bible to read. On Saturday, the fair came to Jacksonville, Florida. My roommate said that he was going to sign up to clean the fair grounds and offered me to sign up too. On October 21, I began working as a member of the clean-up crew every night. One night, I saw this young boy, about twelve years old, carrying a box. When he came up to me, he asked me if I would like a Bible. I didn't think much of it, so, I just told him yes. I asked the young boy how much he wanted for it and he told me that it was free. I insisted that nothing was free and gave him something for it. Surprisingly, he told me that he couldn't take any money for it and said that all the books were inside. I took the Bible, thanked him, and he walked away. When I arrived home, it came back to me that I had just asked Yahawah for a Bible. When I opened the Bible, I sat it on my bed and began reading the first chapter. I fell asleep and the next thing I knew, it was morning and the Bible was laying on my chest.

Jacquelyn, this will be the last story and prediction from your Daddy. In the year of 1951, I worked as a custodian, cleaning up the church grounds for ten years in Mixon Town. As an employee, I got along with the pastor well and felt good about him and the church. I never heard any of his sermons or heard him call on the name of Yahawah, but I did not question these thoughts. One Sunday, Ruby, the kids, and I decided to attend the church I served for so long. There were people standing at the door greeting us, giving us programs, and escorting us to our seats. Everything was going well. The preacher brought a good sermon about loving your neighbors. They took up an offering and the pastor asked all the guest to stand. As I stood, he pointed at me and told me that the yard looked beautiful. I thanked him and then he asked me if I had anything to say. I started off by saying, "Giving honor to the Heavenly Father, Yahawah, and His son, Yahawashi. Giving honor to the pastor and his family, and to every one of you."

The pastor then interrupted me by shouting, "Who was that damn name you said?"

I repeated myself, Yahawah and His son, Yahawashi. Then, the pastor informed me not to call any name unless it was his name. I stated, "Who I serve is who I will call on."

He then said, "You don't call on Jesus Christ's name or Yahawah's name in my church, because those are fake names." I told him that Yahawah and Yahawashi are the real names. The pastor had two men escort me and my family out of the church. The pastor told us to never come back again. Needless to say, we never returned!

CHAPTER 20

DOCUMENTED MATERIALS

Jacquelyn, there are many men who started out serving Yahawah with all their hearts, minds, and souls. Yahawah gave them their heart's desire of money, jobs, beautiful homes, luxury cars, and yet, they were still greedy for more. They built big, beautiful churches for their congregations of hundreds to thousands of members. Yet, they were still unsatisfied and ungrateful. Some of these men and women were seeking wives or husbands, but they were not being careful about whom they selected, just like Solomon. Now you know, Jacquelyn, this is how the devil started possessing these preachers. First, preachers select women from the member's list. Next, they started going on dates with these women, who were supposed to be women of Yahawah. Then, they start sleeping with these women and not being cautious. Outside of the churches, these pastors created their own personal list of women to serve them in and out of bed.

For example, one day, this young energetic pastor decided to pick him a wife without examining her upbringing or values. She captured him with her charm and they were soon married. The next thing you know, she began to super rule over him, telling him what to do. She was even caught going with some of the other ministers in the church. This pastor's wife got pregnant and she was out of control. This all happened, because this pastor craved strange women. It didn't take long before the entire congregation knew his business. What is the lesson to be learned? Can you answer that, Jacquelyn?

I told Daddy that I could. I said, "The pastor should know the Heavenly Father called him to be a preacher, and chose him to become rooted, grounded, and steadfast in Yahawah's word. Yahawah wants to supply our needs every day according to his riches in glory. The pastor should know that the wife is given by God to be a helper to her husband and not a hindrance. Instead of letting money change their thinking, these leaders should have let Yahawah order their lives."

My Daddy responded:

Jacquelyn, you have spoken the truth, my child. Remember, the Israelites became slaves by not obeying Yahawah. We need to learn from our ancestors. When the Israelites had been under the dictatorship of Pharaoh and Rameses, they backslid while living in Egypt. Yet, Yahawah made a way of escape for them. Then, the Israelites made Yahawah so angry that he had to assign an angel to guide them while they were in the wilderness. He did not even want to look upon them. Moses became so angry with them that he disobeyed Yahawah and could not go into the Promised Land. After Moses died in the wilderness, Joshua became their leader and all the older Israelites died out while their young children went into the Promised Land.

CHAPTER 21

HARRIET TUBMAN

In the 1800s, Harriet Tubman was a guide who made the dangerous trip nineteen times, helping over 500 slaves to freedom. Harriet Tubman known for many gifts navigator, mathematician, judge in the wilderness, medicine doctor in the wilderness, meteorologist, excellent swimmer, culinary of survivor of food to eat, a woman walking with Yahawah and his son Yahawashi, ordained evangelist to walk through shadow of death and fear no evil, a few seconds of sleep, deliver babies without proper medical needs while mother and the baby lives, educator taking time to read the bible, building a new life, and resting on the Sabbath Day. Harriet Tubman was an ex-slave who worked under the anointment to the UnderGround Railroad.

The information in this chapter gives insight into the important parts in the early days of African American history. Goree Island is a small forty-five-acre island located off the coast of Senegal. This island was developed as a center for expanding the European slave trade. The first record of slave trading there dates back to 1536 and was conducted by the Portuguese. The first Europeans to set foot on the island were in 1444. The House of Slaves was built in 1776 by the Dutch. This was the last slave house still standing in Goree and now serves as a museum. The island is considered a memorial to the Black Diaspora.

Jacquelyn, the names of these slave countries are called Portugal (Roman Catholic), Saudi Arabia, Spanish colonies of North America, Britain, Europe, Spain, England, France, Hungary, and even the United States, as well as other countries and states.

On September 8, 1565, the oldest city in the United States, Presidio of San Augustin, now called St. Augustine, Florida, had African slaves. Spanish explorer, Pedro Menendez de Aviles, received permission from the king of Spain to import African slaves.

On January 3, 1606, Augustin, son of Augustin and Francisca, was born. He was the first African American to have his birth recorded in the United States. St. Augustine's Church, the Cathedral Basilica, has records dating back to 1594. Some of these are early African American slave records.

On August 20, 1619, John Rolfe, Virginia's first tobacco planter and husband of the princess, Pocahontas, reported the arrival of the first African American slaves in North America by the English. Later, on February 2, 1638, the first American slave ship, Desire, arrived in Massachusetts, having trades of the Pequot Indians for Africans in the West Indies.

In 1641, Massachusetts legalized slavery via Passage 91 in the Body of Liberties, making it the first legal code established by European colonists in New England.

On February 18, 1688, an anti-slavery petition was written by four Quaker men in Germantown. It was the first American document making a plea for equal human rights for everyone. The petition was forgotten until 1844, when it resurfaced to become popular during the abolitionist movement in the United States.

The African Americans will never forget about the transatlantic slave trade that began their voyage in early 1700s by importing cotton, sugar, tobacco, human cargo, guns, alcohol, and metal goods. These products were exchanged for slaves. On the second leg of the voyage is known as the Middle Passage, between Africa and North America. This ship was pacted with African slaves. Merchants made huge profits from this trade in human cargo at the cost of millions of lives.

In 1785, South Carolina's newspaper advertised that the ship under Captain Thomas Morton, called the Commerce, had "upwards of 200 prime slaves" for sale from Africa's Gold Coast.

In 1807, British Parliament abolished the buying and selling of slaves. The Abolition of the Slave Trade Act did not stop slavery, but it stopped the transporting of slaves on ships from Britain. Thanks to abolitionists, the U.S. Congress also passed the law that would later pave the way for the end of slavery.

In 1840, the Act to Prohibit the Importation of Slaves and a similar law was passed in the United Kingdom but was not able to end the slave trade or slavery.

During slavery, there were White people who stood up for us while some were killing us and putting us on plantations all over the world. Our names were changed from the names of Israelites, Ethiopians, Twelve tribes of Judah, and the chosen people. We were called livestock, prime slaves, negroes, niggers, coons, colored, dark skin, the Africans, dumb niggers, monkeys, Black, and African Americans. For a long time, the Gentiles and the White race treated us like animals. They put our males and females in a barn and would beat them until they obeyed and performed sexual acts in the open. When this group of male slaves finished having sex with the female slaves, a group of Whites came in and had sex with the same women.

In addition to sexual abuse, the plantation owners would work these prime slaves around the clock with some having their clothes on, while some had them off.

SLAVERY IN THE MILITARY

In 1935, in Sumpter, South Carolina, a man named April, later changed to Anthony Johnson, was a black slave owner and breeder with sixty-eight slaves. He called his land the

Burrow House Plantation, where these slaves worked and cared for his land.

The livestock journey kept getting worse and worse, which led to being stripped from our inheritance, language, and our true Heavenly Father, Yahawah and His son, Yahawashi.

The Negro race evolved and made life at a different time. We had a few rights and even protested slavery for abolishment. We had the support of many Whites, attorneys to represent us, good jobs, and even higher learning (more than a high school diploma), but we are still in slavery. Our generation is still in slavery of the mind, body, finance, and spirit. However, we are still surviving and standing up for our rights with dignity.

CHAPTER 22

NEW NAME

Black Americans earned a new name by fighting against discrimination, segregation, and systemic problems. They used their backbone and hard work to accomplish their goals. With leaders like Harriet Tubman, who persevered through wild wooded areas, lakes, streams, and rivers to pursue and accomplish the greatest feats in the Underground Railroad, in which millions of slaves were set free. The NAACP (National Association for the Advancement of Colored People) fought for equal rights for Black Americans. The age of new creativity was called the Harlem Renaissance of the 1920s.

In the 1800s, a book called the Black Codes denied African Americans of their basic rights. After slavery was abolished, laws were passed so that all African American voters had to pay a tax and pass a literacy test, just to become a farmer. Hence, they claimed their new name of perseverance.

LIFE OF SLAVERY

Hezekiah Hoodie Rhodes was a blacksmith in 1855. He was chosen from 50 other slaves to get the title of blacksmith. He was paid a White man's salary to do the job. Since only one slave received this honor once per year, Mr. Rhodes made enough money in the blacksmith profession to free those in slavery, they purchased land, and send his family to school. As a result, the Rhodes brothers taught school in the Neyles area for children up to seventh grade. The Rhodes family began to prosper and founded Neyles and the first Presbyterian church. One of his offsprings is the popular local Doctor Harold Rhodes in Walterboro.

Between 1861 and 1865, thousands of African American soldiers fought for the Union. During these four years of bitter fighting, they were still trying to claim their new name.

In 1866, the 14th Amendment gave citizenship and equal rights to all people born in the United States. In 1869, the 15th Amendment gave voting rights to all male U.S. citizens. In 1877, the reconstruction program helped to set Negroes on their feet by giving them land and opportunity. The Freedmen's Bureau set up schools and colleges, which helped freed slaves buy land and find work.

CHAPTER 23

MOVING UP IN MODERN DAY

In 1917, the Harlem Hellfighters, the 15th National Guard African Americans, became soldiers and called themselves the 369th infantry regiment. These young soldiers went into the military ready to fight for the United States as soldiers. The United States had another program for these soldiers to serve as relegators, labour service. They cooked, cleaned, washed dishes, washed uniforms, shined other soldier's boots and buckles, cleaned the outhouse and even served as high rank officials.

Jacquelyn, we continued to move up the ladder with great success becoming congressmen, senators, civil rights leaders like Dr. Martin Luther King Jr, attorneys like Thurgood Marshall and later, the first African American Supreme Court Justice. In the 1960s, the U.S. government passed laws officially ending segregation in public places. We continued to move up the ladder as teachers, professors, doctors, musicians, ballet dancers, book authors like Maya Angelou, actors like James Earl Jones, pastors over Presbyterian churches, and business leaders, including owning our own insurance companies.

Moses Colleton came through a generation of hard persevering people. Moses became the head chef of culinary in 1963 at a restaurant called Maison's Cafeteria in Jacksonville, Florida.

Ben Ammo Ben Israel, who lead the largest movement of African Americans from America to Israel in 1967. The largest movement of African people from one continent to another since 1792. And established an independent African Community that is prospering til this day.

From 1970 to 2000, Luscious Jerome Hester was the president over the entire postal service on Kings Road in Jacksonville, Florida.

In 1995, Annie May Rhodes served as a member of the Colleton County City Council in Walterboro, South Carolina until her untimely death.

In 2011, Elbert Akins III opened the first private Black American barbershop by the name of Headquarters Barbershop on King Street in Jacksonville, Florida.

James Maxie owned his own electric company in Jacksonville, Florida during the years of 1995 through 2017.

Albert and Sheila Frazier opened their own private business called At Your Service Limos in Jacksonville, Florida and has been opened since 2014.

Shiela Martina Keaise is the first African American Children's Librarian at the Colleton County Memorial Library in Walterboro, South Carolina in February 1996. She is an author of over 12 books and is the owner of a publishing company since 2007.

Kelvin Maurice Blufton, Sr. opened the first Vegan Restaurant in South Carolina on May 17, 1999, called The Soul Vegetarian South Restaurant. Using vegetarian instead of vegan in the name help target customers who had problems relating to the term vegan.

Dr. Gail Rearden is a doctor in Walterboro, South Carolina. She has been practicing for many years. She completed her residency at MUSC Hospital in Charleston, South Carolina.

During the years of 2009 through 2016, the first African American president, President Barack Obama, served as the 44th president.

Erika Davis is the author of A man of God, A husband, And a father in 2016.

Dr. Leroy and Helen Polite are authors of 101 Excuses not to come to work in 2017.

Harold M. Rhodes III, D.D.S, has a black private owned business called Colleton Dental Associates in Walterboro, South Carolina.

Abraham Colleton began the apprenticeship program with a line maintainer for Jacksonville City Electric from 1966 - 1996. Abraham Colleton was the second African American male to be hired in Jacksonville, Florida. During this time he passed a test with a very high score. Later, Abraham Colleton insisted inclusion and diversity in his program. As a result, Jacksonville Electric Authority (JEA) became a diverse place of employment for all races.

Ieesha Chandler started her graphic and web design company in March of 2006 working with local companies around the Charleston, South Carolina area. Today, she works with multiple businesses throughout the United States in many different industries.

Jacquelyn Hester Colleton-Akins, Case No: 93-968-Civ-J-20. Sued Duval County School Board. Position as a school teacher in the year 1983 fighting for discrimination.

On November 2020, President Joseph R. Biden became President of the United States.

Kamala Harris became the first African American female Vice President in history in November

CHAPTER 24

MY FATHER'S LAST PREDICTIONS

Jacquelyn, these are my last predictions for you. First of all, you and Abraham will be getting back together in 2004, after you divorce your husband that you are married to now. You will be doing the right thing, because Abraham was your first husband. This time it will work out and I pray you make the right decision. Shalom.

In 303 A.D., Augustus of the East ordered the church and the scriptures to be destroyed. The Christians were deprived of official ranks and priests were imprisoned. Then, he made a decree banning Christians from participating in state sacrifice under the ruling of the church by real ministers. This ban stopped the church congregation from their proper worship and doctrines of Yahawah. The emperor of Constantine the Great created a decree called the Nicene Creed in 325 A.D. The people were forced to call their Father, Jesus Christ, instead of Yahawah. Constantine the Great went to Africa and stopped the ministers and bishops from training young people who wanted to be ministers of Yahawah. During this period, all Christians were persecuted, killed, and placed in a den of animals. The animals killed and ate them. These Christians were shot with bow and arrows and guns like animals. In the early part of Egypt, John the Baptist's head was cut off and other Christians' heads were cut off as well. Just as these things happened, during your time Jacquelyn, you will see the same activity of the killing of Christians. Beware of what is going on and who they are killing the most, the Twelves Tribes of Judah.

In the year 2017, I predict massive killings taking place on the Hebrew people. There will be bombing of churches. (Give the year he prophesied this or other words)

Jacquelyn, keep in mind that you will see the end times every day you live, and it will get worse. You will get a chance to see the Antichrist come into his full power, and you will be called home. Your job is to preach, teach, and live the life of the Heavenly Father, Yahawah, and his son, Yahawashi.

My final words to all:

I forgave Adam and Eve and I will forgive everyone that came up against me and all the Ethiopians and the Twelve Tribes of Judah. I pray for them to receive Yahawah and Yahawashi as their savior. Jacquelyn, the time is 6:00 am and it is time for you to turn off the recorder because your husband is at the hotel and so are your children.

That morning in 1978, I asked Daddy if he would like some breakfast or some fruit. He told me to just buy three jugs of apple juice and a cup with a lid. We purchased what he requested and took him back to his rooming house. I helped him out of the car and he hugged and kissed my forehead and said goodbye. I observed Daddy climb the steps very weakly, but he had a glow in his face as he turned around and gave me his Bible. I stood there for a moment crying and saw my Daddy for the last time for he died four days later. I got into my automobile and drove to the hotel to meet my family. Daddy never went into another church but was buried in a Jehovah's Witness church, not by his choice, but my mother's.

Pilate condemned Yahawashi to death. Yahawashi was led to Calvary but on his way, a great company, including women bewailed and lamented him, he stopped and turned unto them and said, *Daughters of Jerusalem, weep not for me, but weep for yourselves and for your children. (St. Luke 23:29). For behold, the days are coming, in which they shall say, Blessed are the barren, and wombs that never bare, and the paps which never gave suck (St. Lukes 23:26-27).* Daddy prophesied these scriptures when young Hebrew men and women were being sold in slave auctions in a place called Libya. He said this will occur in the years of 1990s through 2018 and beyond.

WHAT YAHAWAH REVEALED TO ME

We as African Americans are living in a very confusing system, being taught one way, then later finding there is another way. I am finding out our world we live in has kept one of the biggest secrets to themselves. The big secret was that Blacks were denied knowing the Heavenly Father and his son (Yahawah and Yahawashi), language, the sin that we brought upon ourselves, dialect, culture, true history, religion, and where we came from. So, they can rise to the top and be over everything in this world. What does it profit a man to gain all the richness of life, live in fine houses, be head on the job, and make the laws of the land, but ultimately lose his soul? The Holy Bible teaches us to study, seek, knock, and pray for wisdom, knowledge, and understanding in our walk of life. Adam and Eve, the Ethiopians, committed the first sin by being disobedient to the Heavenly Father to the laws of the land. Just as Yahawah forgive Adam and Eve for what they had done, he forgave everyone that came up against me in my life with persecution, discrimination, lying, and stealing. He even forgave them from taking the Bible, causing harm, and blatantly persecuting the Ethiopian race.

Over the years, I kept going back adding to this book waiting for my Daddy's prophecy to come to past. My Daddy's prophecy came true because the Ethiopians, Mexicans, Hispanics, Chineses, Indians, Puerto Ricans, Columbia Indians, American Indians, Jamaicans, Myans, Dominican Republicans, and Haitian Christians are being persecuted, because they are Hebrews, Yahawah's Twelve Tribes of the Nation of Israel. Mass murderers have over populated the earth, killing Hebrew people everywhere. The enemy is doing the same thing from the past to right now in 2017. There is nothing new under the sun.

Yahawah and His son is looking upon the earth and know that it is corrupted, sinful, and massively violent. Some of the Hebrews are serving pagan gods and not obeying the commandments and statutes that were given to them from the beginning. Yahawah will soon come to destroy the earth with fire. The Bible made this statement.

Daddy's prophecy about my marriage came true, too. Elbert and I divorced, and Abraham and I united and raised our grandchildren. We are now living in South Carolina as a happy family. The world has not come to an end yet, but it soon will. By Yahawah's grace, when I pass away, my granddaughter Marilyn Colleton will continue this book. The only thing did not come to past yet from Daddy's prophecy is the Anti-Christ gaining full power on earth.

Yahuwah will clean up all this sinful behavior that has been going on from the beginning. Yahawah said in His word what is crooked will remain crooked until he returns in the cloud. LOOK OUT all you fearful unbelievers, perverts, murderers, whoremongers, sorcerers, idolaters, and liars. You will have your part in the lake that burns with fire and brimstones, which is the second death. The Bible says that the earth will not be destroyed by water, but by fire. I asked the Heavenly Father to forgive me of my sins in Yahawashi's name. I pray for forgiveness of anyone who comes up against me. Shalom.

CHAPTER 25

THE TEN COMMANDMENTS

The Ten Commandments are the first ten of six hundred and thirteen commandments given by Yahawah to the Hebrew people. Yahawah gave Moses the Ten Commandments on the Mountain of Mount Sinai. *(Exodus 3:1;4:27;18:5)*

The Ten Commandments are:

1. I am Yahawah, who brought thee out of the land of Egypt, out of the house of bondage.
2. Thou shalt have no other gods before me.
3. Thou shalt not take the name of Yahawah in vain.
4. Remember the Sabbath day to keep it holy.
5. Honor thy father and thy mother.
6. Thou shalt not kill.
7. Thou shalt not commit adultery.
8. Thou shalt not steal.

9. Thou shalt not bear false witness against thy neighbor.
10. Thou shalt not covet anything that belongs to thy neighbor.

CHAPTER 26

THE ANCIENT HISTORY OF ETHIOPIANS

The Tribes of Israel were additional divisions of the ancient Hebrew Ethiopian people. Their biblical tradition holds the foundation of our Christian background in Yahawah's tabernacle. Abraham, Isaac, and Jacob are our Hebrew forefathers, which consist of fathers, sons, and grandsons. The name Jacob was given by Yahawah. The Israelites were fertile and prolific. They multiplied and increased greatly. They became the "Israelite people" after the death of Joseph. In Egypt, Pharaoh and Rameses oppressed the Ethiopian Israelites by placing them under burdensome labor and annihilating the male babies. Yahawah made a covenant with Abraham, Isaac, and Jacob by making himself known to Moses and rescuing the Israelites from Egypt. The Ethiopian nation numbered 600,000 men, women, children, and animals as they walked out of Egypt and into the wilderness.

The Egyptian pyramids are ancient pyramid-shaped masonry structures located in Egypt. As of November 2008, sources cite either 118 or 138 as the number of identified Egyptian pyramids. Most were built as tombs for the country's pharaohs and their consorts during the Old and Middle Kingdom periods.

THE TWELVE TRIBES OF ISRAEL (IN ALPHABETICAL ORDER):

1. Asher - Columbian Plymouth Rock Indians
2. Benjamin - West Indies and Caribbean Island
3. Dan - Remained in the ship beyond the Jordan River
4. Ephraim - The great oasis at Kadesh-Barnea where the tribe remained
5. Gad - Native American Indians
6. Issachar - Fought against the King of Am-lek
7. Joseph - After his death, the people's name changed to the Israelites

8. Judah - American Negroes/Black Americans
9. Levi - Haitians
10. Napthali - His death was in the field, fighting the King of Canaan
11. Rueben - Seminole Indians
12. Simeon - Dominican Republicans

CHAPTER 27

INSTRUCTIONS ON HOW TO BE SUCCESSFUL

1. You must pray and read the bible every day. Read the King James Version or one of the Bibles that include all the books. Recite Yahawah's prayer three times daily. (St. Matthews 6:9 - 13)

2. You must be born again. (Romans 10:9 - 17)

3. You must live the life as Yahawashi did, and obey the words from the Bible. (Leviticus 26:3 - 5)

4. You must seek the Heavenly Father and His son's wisdom, knowledge, and understanding. You will be in this world, but be careful not to participate in any sinful acts of serving pagan gods and traditions of this world. (John 3:16 - 33)

5. You must present yourself holy and acceptable to Yahawah and Yahawashi. (Romans 12:1 - 8)

6. You must be kind and affectionate to one another with brotherly love. (Romans 12:9 - 21)

> Note: It is good to say I'm sorry for any mistake you have done or you have done to the heavenly father.

7. You must understand who has power over this world.
8. Now you are ready to receive the Holy Ghost and be baptized. (Romans 15:13 - 15)
9. You must walk daily in your new life. You no longer belong to Satan and this world. (Leviticus 26:1 - 8)

> Note: Always remember not to take part in their customs of idolatry and to never pray to their pagan gods. Be careful what church or synagogue you assemble yourself. Be careful what Bible you are reading and the company you keep in the church or on your professional job.

10. Yahawah holy, which is the sixth day. You must not work on this day.

> Note: Saturday is the sabbath day, not Sunday.

11. Yahawashi was in the ground for three days (Wednesday, Thursday, and Friday) (Exodus 20:10 - 21). Keep in mind you must work for six days. For example: You may cook, clean and prepare the sabbath day meal, including shewbread and not Subway's bread. (Exodus 20:5 - 9)

> Note: The whole family, men, women, and children, should do all their work before the Sabbath Day, so that they can rest.

12. You must keep the three feasts. (Exodus 23:14 - 19)

13. You must obey and keep his commandments and his statues every day and night. (Exodus 20:1 - 17; Deuteronomy 28:1 - 68)

> Note: This includes the whole family without exceptions.

CHAPTER 28

CONCLUSION

The Heavenly Father and His son asked you to remember how the Israelite people made the golden calf to worship when Moses went up to Mount Sinai. When Moses did not return within a certain time, the people lost focus of who was the true and living Yahuwah.

Adam and Eve disobeyed Yahawah's commandments from the beginning. Sin prevailed and soon the Israelites sinned against Yahawah again. The Ethiopian Israelite people went through a lot of persecution in Egypt as a result of their disobedience. They ended up in the wilderness, but was still practicing the deeds of Egyptians, like worshipping and serving a false dead god.

Today, this is the meaning of each part of the golden calf. The head of the calf represents all of the churches in the world. The neck of the calf represents who is in control of these churches. The shoulders and front legs of the calf represents all the people in this world that lead the world's resources like businesses, the government, hospitals, law enforcement, the FBI, educators, retailers, etc. The body from the shoulders to the butt and the hind legs represent how the government agencies take care of the different races in the world, whether they be rich, poor, handicapped, normal or government assisted. The tail represents all Christian people, like the twelve tribes, the Israelites, and other Christian Hebrews serving Yahawah and Yahawashi.

All of mankind living on earth should remember the beginning when Adam and Eve failed to obey Yahawah, choosing the Tree of Knowledge of Good and Evil instead of the Tree of Life. When you begin studying and examining the Bible with all of the books, please do not disregard the King James Version. You will need all the information from this version. The Ethiopian race recognize Yahawah, because he put us into slavery due to the disobedience of His commandments and statutes. I have discovered the earth has been created thousands of times and more. Adam and Eve chose the wrong tree each time. When I read Deuteronomy 28:67 - 68, I'm reminded of these words, *Yahawah shall bring thee into Egypt again with ships, by the way whereof I spoke to thee, thou shalt see it no more again, and there you will be sold unto your enemies for bondmen and bond women, and no man will buy you.*

I have the faith of a mustard seed and believe that one day, four hundred years will be over for the Hebrew and Israelite people. We have served the Gentiles and had their children. We were called by the name livestock and yet, we still served them well throughout our lives on this earth. So, each day I look to the hills to where my health and strength come from to survive on this earth. Before we became integrated, our school books had language written with red and black poisoned pens to keep our minds in bondage. I remembered to look beyond the poisoned pen writing and engulf myself in what the author had to tell me in the book.

HEALING FROM ABOVE

a. On December 13, 1993, I had a doctor's appointment concerning the area underneath my arms, the armpits. They were always sore, and I struggled to find the proper deodorant to use for my body type. The doctor took tests and later performed a biopsy. The results came back positive and I was informed that I was in the second stage of breast cancer. I left the doctor's office and travelled to the park. I just sat at the fountain where the water shoots up and then later moved to watch the river. I had no one to talk to except the Heavenly Father and His son, so I just cried for hours. I remembered when my parents told me that when the bad gets worse, that's when you have faith in who you are serving. Then, right in that moment, I heard a soft voice and it was my Daddy's voice. As I looked all around, I knew my Daddy had passed away, but I still heard his voice. "Pray to Yahawah and walk and have faith no matter what is going on in your life. Always believe you are healed and have faith in the words of Yahawah and Yahawashi. Jacquelyn, you are only going through a test." Then, I felt a cool breeze of air all over me. On October 19, 1994, Yahawah healed me from the cancer.

For twenty years, I struggled with my problem under my arms and no one seemed to care or understand, but Marilyn, my granddaughter. On October 4, 2017, I woke up feeling refreshed and I heard a watery voice tell me to use Marilyn's deodorant. Once I put the deodorant underneath my arms, I haven't used any other deodorant since October 4, 2017, to December 13, 1993 and have no complaints. I waited for Yahawah's time to be healed and He was right on time.

b. Elbert, my son, broke his right femur bone while playing football in middle school. He was rushed to Baptist Hospital in Jacksonville, Florida. Dr. Eric Loveless, MD tended to his emergency and ordered an x–ray of his right leg. During this time, Elbert was in severe pain because the femur bone broke in half. He kept hollering out, "Jesus, Jesus save my leg". Dr. Loveless suggested that they put him to sleep because he had a cyst in his leg, and we were waiting for the results to come back from the lab. The doctor explained to us just what the laboratory report stated and he said, "Your son has cancer in the third stage."

I broke down and went on my knees in the presence of a lot of people in the emergency room, speaking in Hebrew. The doctor stated that he needed surgery immediately. At 4:45 am, they took Elbert to surgery. However, when they got into surgery and cut his leg open, they found no cyst. They read the x – ray again and called the pathologist. He stated there was a large cyst there and the doctors carried on with their conversation, trying to find out what happened. Later, they came to tell us at 6:05 am that the cyst was gone and there was just a hollow hole there in his right leg. The doctors said that they took more x-rays of what they observed, and they put his bone back together with a rod used in a spaceship (NASA) and they flew in a bone specialist to come in and observed their findings. All the doctors, along with Dr. Loveless, agreed that this was a miracle from the Heavenly Father, Yahawah.

Our son loved playing sports. He played basketball, football, and was drafted for basketball by Success Academy Private School. However, after this miracle, Elbert decided to turn down the position to play basketball. He felt that the requirements for this sport would cause him to lose his core values. Elbert wanted to live his life for the work of Yahawashi instead. Even though he never had any more problems with his leg again, Elbert knew if he played professionally, he would be required to go and do things that would jeopardize his relationship with Yahawah. He knew that basketball would require playing, practicing, and going to events on Saturdays, the sabbath. Elbert thanks Yahawah and his son Jesus Christ/Yahawashi every day for his many blessings. He has no regrets.

Daniel was born in 1999, with thirty five medical illnesses in his body. His diagnoses were premature baby, fetal alcohol syndrome, cerebral palsy, Neuromuscular scoliosis of lumbosacral region, to name a few. Daniel's body was turning from front to back. Daniel parent's brought him to MUSC hospital in Charleston, South Carolina. James F. Mooney, MD, who specializes in orthopaedic surgery, operated on Daniel in the year 2015, this operation was successful in Yahawah's name. The doctors in Jacksonville, Florida said he would never walk, talk, and grow to a normal size human. At MUSC hospital Daniel is receiving physical therapy and under the care of Dr. Stephen Kinsman MD, for botox for spastic diplegia and cerebral palsy. Daniel is human size and Dr. Kinsmans is treating Daniel for muscle spasms and muscle tension. Dr. Kinsman, came into Daniel's examination room on the first floor at Rutledge Tower with a new kind of bedside manner. He introduced a different kind of examining with music to Daniel and he just opened up to Dr. Kinsman and began moving all kinds of different ways. Daniel had a look of joy and loved Dr. Kinsman examination. For three years Daniel looked forward to interacting with Dr. Kinsman and having his examinations. I believe Dr. Kinsman was used by Yahawah to break down Daniel barriers of not liking doctors. Now, Daniel has been different attitude toward doctors and being examined by them. Daniel began growing a keloid on his left shoulder. Dr. M. Lance Tavana, MD, and his internal doctors worked with Daniel to dissolve his keloid by injections. Today, Daniel is mentally retarded and unable to verbalize. He needs a wheelchair to go long distance and sometimes short distance. Daniel will never be able to take care of himself, but me and my family and I will gladly take care of Daniel.

Today, Daniel stands at 5'4, with beautiful hair on his head. Daniel is walking with help. He can even run, jump, and bend his knees. His favorite sport to play with help is soccer. Daniel may have been in a profound class in high school, but he graduated on May 6, 2017 with his big brother Raymond walking him down the line. Daniel still have seizures and cannot feed himself properly, but he is still going on in Yahawah name. Daniel is receiving speech therapy at MUSC hospital from Samantha McDonald, SLP. With his love of travel and gospel music, Daniel is very happy. His biological mother or father may not have been there, but his sister Marilyn, his brother Raymond, his two grandfathers, grandmother, his favorite cousin Jabbari Williams-El, and his favorite uncles, Alex and Elbert will always be there assisting their nephew with love and care in Yahawah's name.

HEBREW CALENDAR

The Hebrew calendar was under the name of Rosh Hashanah, at the beginning of time when the heavenly father Yahawah created mankind.

CONSTELLATIONS

Chronology was a chief consideration in the study of astronomy among the Jews; sacred time was based upon the cycles of the Sun and the Moon. The Talmud identified the twelve constellations of the zodiac with the twelve months of the Hebrew calendar. The correspondence of the constellations with their names in Hebrew and the months is as follows:

1. **Aries** – Taleh – **Nisan**
2. **Taurus** – Shor – **Iyar**
3. **Gemini** – Teomim – **Sivan**
4. **Cancer** – Sartan – **Tammuz**
5. **Leo** – Arye – **Av**

6. **Virgo** – Betulah – **Elul**
7. **Libra** – Moznayim – **Tishrei**
8. **Scorpio** – 'Akrab – **Marcheshvan**
9. **Sagittarius** – Keshet – **Kislev**
10. **Capricorn** – Gdi – **Tevet**
11. **Aquarius** – Dli – **Shevat**
12. **Pisces** – Dagim – Adar

THE YEAR IN HEBREW

The Hebrew calendar year conventionally begins on Rosh Hashanah. However other dates serves as the beginning of the year for different religious purpose later, they changed the months, dates, days of the week, and the time due to religious festivities and national holidays. However the ancient slaves was unable to speak or teach this information to their offspring or family. Moving down through a timeline the new slaves was unable to receive this information due to slaves was not suppose to learn how to read, write, or speak Hebrew. The year 5778 since the creation of the world, according to the additional count.

- This year has 354 days, making it a regular (כסדרה) year.
- In 5778, Rosh Hashanah is on Thursday, while Passover is on Saturday.

NAMES OF THE WEEK DAY

1. Sunday — Yom Rishon
2. Monday — Yom Sheni
3. Tuesday — Yom Shlishi
4. Wednesday — Yom Revi'i
5. Thursday — Yom Chamishi
6. Friday — Yom Shishi
7. Saturday — Yom Shabbat

HEBREW MONTHS

Shevat – January/February

Adar – February/March

Nisan – March/April

Iyar – April/May

Sivan – May/June

Tammuz – June/July

Av – July/August

Elul – August/September

Tishrei – September/October

Heshvan – October/November

Kislev – November/December

Tevet – December/January

VOCABULARY TERMS

(IN ALPHABETICAL ORDER)

1. Abraham – an Old Testament patriarch regarded by Jews as the founder of the Hebrew people through his son Isaac and by Muslims as the founder of the Arab people through his son Ishmael.
2. Adam – Ayekah
3. Angels – a spiritual being superior to humans in power and intelligence.
4. Armageddon - A war between The Heavenly Father and Lucifer
5. Bible – build the Christian scriptures, consisting of the Old and New Testaments.
6. Bona – real, authentic, and genuine.
7. Bone marrow - Bone marrow is the spongy tissue inside some of the bones in the body, including the hip, thigh, and rib. Bone marrow contains immature cells, called stem cell, bone marrow donation. The first is a bone marrow donation which involves the removal of bone marrow from the male rib Adam

8. Constantine – Emperor of Rome who started the persecution of Christians in 303 A.D made Christianity the official religion of the Roman Empire.

9. Creation - the bringing into of existence of the - heaven and earth, especially when regarded as an act of The Heavenly Father.

10. DNA – chromosome (male x – y) (female x – x) – deoxyribonucleic acid

11. Dust – fine, dry powder consisting of tiny particles of earth or waste matter lying on the ground or on surfaces or carried in the air.

12. Egypt – country in northeastern Africa.

13. Enoch – A Hebrew patriarch, father of Methuselah.

14. Ethiopians – a native or inhabitant of Ethiopia,

15. Eve – Chare

16. Exile – going into captivity

17. Fall – sin

18. Formed – Man – ish

19. Garden of Eden – In the Holy bible a place where Adam, Eve, a lot of animals, plants, and the Euphrates River is located.

20. Giant – Large children of the Heavenly Father from Heaven or having abilities of supernatural power.

21. Ham – the youngest son of Noah.

22. Hebrew – a member of an ancient people living in what is now Israel and Palestine and, according to biblical tradition, descended from the patriarch Jacob, grandson of Abraham. After the Exodus (c. 1300 BC)

they established the kingdoms of Israel and Judah, and their scriptures and traditions form the basis of the Jewish religion.

23. Idolatry – the worship of idols.
24. Intercourse - communication or dealings between individuals or groups.
25. Into a woman – le -ish – sha
26. Japeth – is one of the three sons of Noah in the Book of Genesis.
27. Jesus - the son of the Heavenly Father who was crucified and he who died for our sins and he shall and will return very soon
28. Kama - Saul
29. Man – ish – formed (squeeing - yachts)
30. Moses – Hebrew prophet who led the Israelites out of Egypt and delivered the Law during their years of wandering in the wilderness.
31. Murder – the unlawful premeditated killing of one human being by another.
32. Mysticism – awakening
33. Nager – tempter
34. Naha – In the garden
35. Naked - Arum
36. **Nicene Creed - In 303 A.D. Augustus of the East ordered the church and scriptures to be destroyed. The Christians were deprived of official ranks, and priests were imprisoned. Then, he made a decree banning Christians from participating**

in state sacrifice under the ruling of the church by real ministers. This ban stopped the church congregation from their proper worship and doctrines of Yahaweh. Emperor Constantine the Great created a decree called the Nicene Creed in 325 A.D The people were forced to call their Father, Jesus Christ, instead of Yahweh, Constantine the Great went to Africa and stopped the ministers and bishops from training young people who wanted to be ministers of Yahweh.

37. Rameses II- is the son of Seti I who became an Egyptian Pharaoh in his 30th year of age. He ruled Egypt for about 67 years. He was believed to be the greatest and the most renowned pharaoh of Egypt. As the 3rd Egyptian pharaoh of the new kingdom, he ruled Egypt from 1279 BC to 1213 BC.

38. Noah – instructed by Yahaweh to build an Ark for Noah's family and pairs of animals and birds before God sent the great flood, and the world began anew.

39. Pyramid- a monumental structure with a square or triangular base and sloping sides that meet in a point at the top, especially one built of stone as a royal tomb in ancient Egypt.

40. Rib – etth – Hassela

41. Serpent - Nachash

42. Shem - was one of the sons of Noah.

43. Shift/changing – A shift is a change in something or an adjustment in the way something is done.

44. Side by side – together

45. Ten plagues – ten disasters inflicted on Egypt by the God of Israel in order to force the Pharaoh to allow the Israelites to depart from slavery.

46. The first Sabbath – a day of religious observance and abstinence from work, kept by Jewish people from Friday evening to Saturday evening, and by most Christians on Sunday.

47. The Ten Commandments – are a set of biblical principles relating to ethics and worship that play a fundamental role in Judaism and Christianity.

48. The tree of knowledge – good and evil

49. Tree of life - Tree that Yahaweh wanted Adam and Eve to eat from to live forever.

50. Twelve tribes of Judah – They were Asher, Dan, Ephraim, Gad, Issachar, Manasseh, Naphtali, Reuben, Simeon, Zebulun, Judah and Benjamin.

51. Twelve tribes of the nation of Israel – Reuben, Simeon, Judah, Issachar, Zebulun, Benjamin, Dan, Naphtali, Gad, Asher, Ephraim and Manasseh.

52. Twins – one of two children or animals born at the same birth.

53. War – a state of armed conflict between different nations or states or different groups within a nation or state.

54. Way – yiven

55. Woman – ishals – built

56. Womb – man

57. Yahawashi – son

58. Yahweh - The Heavenly Father

DADDY'S FAVORITE SONG

"I'M A NOBODY"

I'm a nobody, I'm a nobody trying to tell the people in this world About the Most High Yahawah and his son, Yahawashi.

The father sent his son Yahawashi into this world to die for all mankind.

I'm a nobody because, I am a victim in sin drinking alcohol for forty years O I'm JUST A NOBODY. Living in the street in Allis off Davis Street.

One night, I became so intoxicated of alcohol I stumbled in this ally and two men beat me up, beat me up, I'm just a nobody.

I managed to pull myself up to get on my knees, I called out on Yahawah. I kept on calling him and I said, I'm just a nobody asking you Yahawashi to save me, save my soul, please, please, please, please, have mercy on me because, I can't live like this anymore.

I'm just a nobody. Yahawashi, save me please...

Me Peter, Me Peter, Me Peter in your Holy name Yahawashi.

THE END